THE TRUTH ABOUT MY UNBELIEVABLE SCHOOL...

For Naomi, Debbie,
Benjamin—best band ever.
—Davide

For Naomi
—Benjamin

Text copyright © 2018 by Davide Cali.
Illustrations copyright © 2018 by Benjamin Chaud.

Library of Congress Cataloging-in-Publication Data available.

ISBN 978-1-4521-5594-4

Manufactured in China.

Design by Ryan Hayes.
Typeset in 1820 Modern.

10 9 8 7 6 5 4 3 2 1

Chronicle Books LLC
680 Second Street
San Francisco, California 94107

Chronicle Books—we see things differently.
Become part of our community at www.chroniclekids.com.

THE TRUTH ABOUT MY UNBELIEVABLE SCHOOL...

Davide Cali   Benjamin Chaud

chronicle books · san francisco

Henry, would you please show your new classmate around our school today?

Well, there really isn't much to see . . .
Maybe you'd like to feed the class pet?

This is the music room. The teacher is pretty good.

And here is the art room. Do you like to paint?

Welcome to the math corner.
It's okay if you don't understand the equation . . .

nobody does.

The science room is this way.
We're working on a secret experiment . . .

It's almost finished.

The hall gets a little wild during recess.

Let's take a shortcut . . .

There really isn't
anything to see here.

This is the gym.
Our P.E. teacher is an Olympic champion.

But our swimming instructor is kind of strange.

Are you hungry?
The cafeteria food
isn't too bad.

But sometimes there are problems with the mashed potatoes.

As you can see, our library is huge . . .
Sometimes kids get lost in here!

This is the teacher's lounge.
Nobody knows what goes on inside.

Hey! Where are you going? That's the janitor's closet!

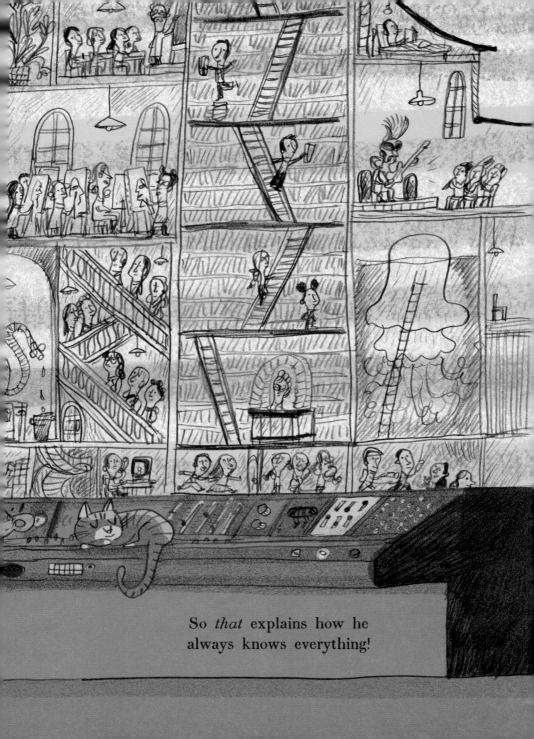

So *that* explains how he
always knows everything!

Be very quiet.

And here we are . . . the principal's office!

She seems busy
at the moment.

We're just in time!

Are you taking
the bus with us?

No, my mom's
picking me up . . .

- The End -

Davide Cali has published more than 40 books, including *A Funny Thing Happened on the Way to School . . .*, *The Truth About My Unbelievable Summer . . .*, *A Funny Thing Happened at the Museum . . .*, and *I Didn't Do My Homework Because . . .*, which has been translated into 21 languages. He lives in France and Italy.

Benjamin Chaud has illustrated more than 60 books, including *I Didn't Do My Homework Because . . .*, *A Funny Thing Happened on the Way to School . . .*, *The Truth About My Unbelievable Summer . . .*, and *A Funny Thing Happened at the Museum. . . .* He lives in Die, France.